The Red Car

by Bobby Lynn Maslen
pictures by John R. Maslen

Scholastic Inc.

New York • Toronto • London • Auckland • Sydney • Mexico City • New Delhi • Hong Kong

Available Bob Books®:

<u>Level A</u>: Set 1 - First!   Set 2 - Fun!

<u>Level B</u>: Set 1 - Kids!   Set 2 - Pals!

<u>Level C</u>: Set 1 - Wow!

Ask for Bob Books at your local bookstore, visit www.bobbooks.com, or call: 1-800-733-557

ISBN 0-439-17563-1

12 11   4 5/0
Printed in China.   08

Barb had a red car.

The red car ran.
The car was a star.

"Hop in, Mark. Hop in, Carl," said Barb.

But the red car did not start.

Mark hopped out.
Carl hopped out.

Barb sat in the car.

"We will push the car,"
said Mark and Carl.

Carl pushed. Mark pushed.

The car started.

Mark and Carl hopped in.
"Smart!" said Barb.

"Rum, rum, rum," said the car.
"Honk, honk," said the horn.

Barb, Mark, and Carl sped off in the red car.

The End

List of 30 words in *The Red Car*

Short Vowels

a	o	i	e	u	irregular
sat	not	in	red	but	a
had	hop	did	sped	rum	the
ran	honk	will			we
and					off
					out
					said
					horn
					push

a as in car

was	Carl
car	star
Barb	start
Mark	smart

85 total words in *The Red Car*